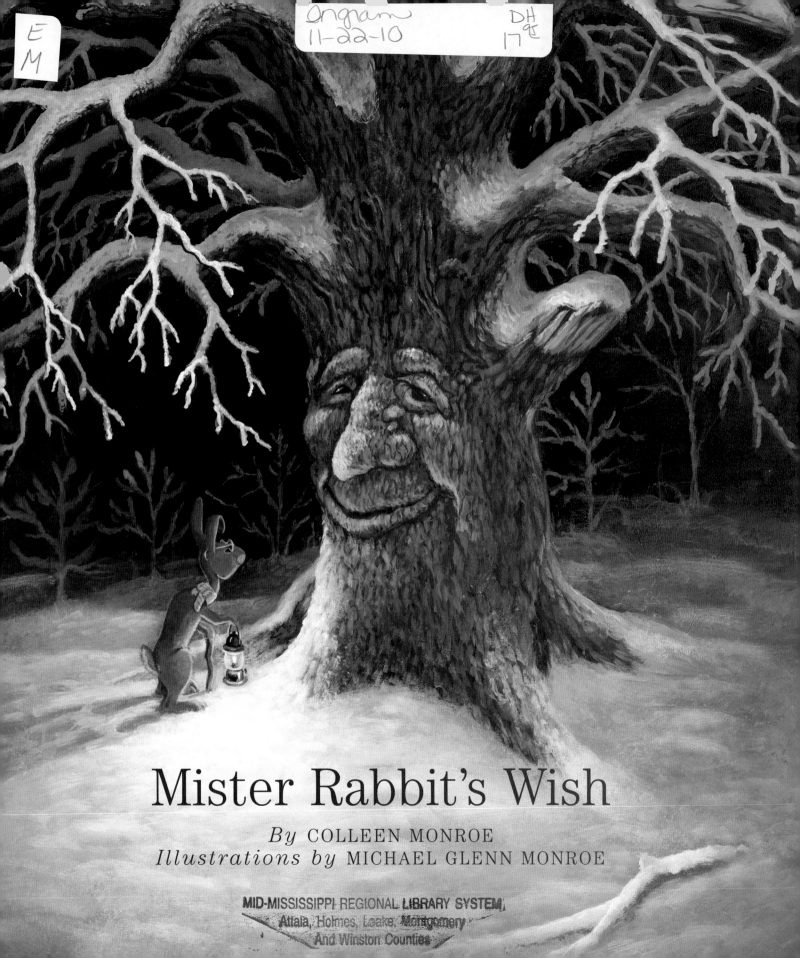

Mister Rabbit's Wish

By COLLEEN MONROE

Illustrations by MICHAEL GLENN MONROE

The old rabbit emerged from his home into the soft evening
light. A fresh coat of sparkling snow covered everything around
him. He leaned on his walking stick as he gazed around the forest
that he loved.

For the old rabbit, this was the most special night of the year. It was
time for him to walk to the Wishing Tree. He had taken this walk every
year at the beginning of winter since he was a small bunny. He smiled as
he remembered his first journey so long ago. It was now much harder for
him to make the walk, but the excitement of seeing the Wishing Tree
again gave his tired, old body new energy.

He started out surrounded by the happy sounds of the forest life around him. The first animal he came upon was his neighbor, Mr. Squirrel.

"Evening Mr. Rabbit, where are you off to tonight?"

"I am off to the Wishing Tree," said Mr. Rabbit.

"The Wishing Tree, what is that?" asked Mrs. Squirrel, who had joined her husband.

"One night a year, a wonderful event happens in the forest. A lone tree, older than the forest itself, grants wishes to those who ask," explained Mr. Rabbit.

"Oh, how wonderful," said the squirrels together. "Would it be alright if we joined you?"

So off the threesome went, making their way deeper into the forest.

It was not long until they ran into Mr. Fox.
"Where are you three off to this fine winter's eve?" asked the fox.
The squirrels went on to tell him the story of the Wishing Tree.

"I would like to join you if you wouldn't mind," said Mr. Fox.
"I would love to ask for a bigger den."

As they continued on through the snow-covered forest, they were joined by many other animals, each intrigued by the thought of a tree that could grant wishes.

"I'm going to wish for more acorns," said Mrs. Squirrel.

"I think I'll wish for a nice birdhouse," chirped the cardinal.

"I'm going to use my wish for a piece of cheese," squeaked the little mouse.

The only one not to speak was the old rabbit. He had wished for the same thing every year since he had first made the walk to the Wishing Tree. This year would be no different.

By now night had fallen in the woods and stars could be seen peeking through the branches above. The light from the moon reflected through the trees, giving the snow a soft, bluish glow.

They walked until they came to a small clearing in the middle of the forest. Here the air was silent and calm.

"Are we there?" whispered the skunk.

"Which tree is it?" the deer quietly asked.

"It must be the one there in the middle," murmured the pheasant.

They all turned to look at what must surely be the most beautiful tree in the forest. It stood tall and proud. Its strong branches were covered with glistening snow.

At first the animals were so busy gazing
upon the tree they didn't notice the old rabbit
had continued walking past the large spruce.

Instead, he stopped in front of an old oak tree.
Its trunk was scarred and its thick branches
had been broken off in spots. After a moment,
the others followed him as he hobbled close
to the old tree, reaching out to stroke its
battered bark as he softly spoke to it.

It seemed to the other animals that the tree turned toward
them and bowed its branches. Then the tree began to speak.

"Welcome, new friends, I'm glad you are here.
To tell me your wishes, you'll have to draw near.

"Speak to me clearly your wish from the heart,
but first I should warn you before we can start ...

"I can only grant wishes that are kind and are true,
So make sure that your wishes aren't centered on you.

"The evening draws late and it's time we began.
Step forward my friends, and I'll do what I can."

Mr. Rabbit motioned them forward one at a time to
lay their paws and wings upon the rough bark of the trunk.
Each animal was filled with excitement as it touched the tree and
spoke its wish. Mr. Rabbit stood by as each asked for bigger homes, more
food, and other things.

Finally, it was the old rabbit's turn. He spoke his wish so softly that it could only be heard by the Wishing Tree. He then put his arms as far as they could go around the tree trunk and hugged his old friend good-bye. With that, he turned to make the long walk home.

At first, all the animals silently followed Mr. Rabbit, deep in thought about their wishes. Then, all at once, they began talking excitedly about what it would be like if their wishes actually came true.

"Won't it be wonderful to have all the things we wished for?" asked Mr. Fox.

"Oh, I can't wait to get home and see if it's really true!" said Mrs. Squirrel.

Finally, Mr. Squirrel noticed that Mr. Rabbit hadn't spoken and asked, "So, what was your wish, Mr. Rabbit?"

After a moment of silence Mr. Rabbit spoke. "I have walked to the Wishing Tree and made the same wish since I was a young bunny …
I wish for Peace on Earth."

"But you have wasted your wish every year," all the animals cried. "Why do you still make the long walk for nothing?"

The old rabbit stood silent, leaning on his walking stick for a moment before he spoke.

"Don't you understand that every year I have been given one of the greatest gifts?" he softly said. "The Wishing Tree has given me the gift of hope. The Wishing Tree has told me that one year, when more than just one old bunny wishes for peace, that he will have the strength to grant my wish."

The others stood silently as each thought of the selfish
wish that they had made for themselves. They realized the wisdom
of the old rabbit and longed to take their wishes back and change them.
They turned to apologize to Mr. Rabbit for their selfishness.

　　He smiled kindly on them all and said, "Now you see why I take
the long walk. It is such a small price to pay for such a wish."

　　With that he hobbled away, leaning on his walking stick,
making the long journey home.

To my sister Michele
who believes in
the power of all wishes,
big and small.
—CM

All inquiries should be addressed to:
Mitten Press, An imprint of Ann Arbor Media Group LLC, 2500 S. State Street, Ann Arbor, MI 48104

CPSIA tracking label information: Printed and bound in Guangdong, China
Date of Production: 08/15/2009
Cohort: Batch 1

10 9 8 7 6 5 4 3 2 1

Library of Congress Cataloging Data on File.

ISBN: 978-1-58726-525-9